A Goblin's Desire

Johanna Stockall

Introduction: A Goblin's Desire

In the heart of a bustling metropolis, where the symphony of life played its cacophonous tune, an unlikely protagonist emerged. Grumble, a goblin with a heart that beat with dreams untamed, found himself navigating the labyrinthine alleys and towering spires of the city.

One fateful night, the tapestry of fate unfurled before him, revealing a figure cloaked in shadows and grace. Clara, a homeless woman with eyes that held the glint of forgotten strength, stood at the crossroads of destiny. Their worlds, seemingly worlds apart, collided in an encounter that would ignite a tale woven with threads of magic, love, and transformation.

As Grumble's heart stirred with a burning desire to change Clara's fate, he delved into the depths of his arcane powers. His nimble fingers wove spells that danced in the moonlight, stealing from the shadows to bring prosperity to his newfound muse. The city's underbelly became his clandestine playground, every venture a daring dance on the precipice of danger.

Yet, amidst the city's ceaseless clamor, Clara remained oblivious to the mystical forces at play. Unbeknownst to her, Grumble watched over her, a silent guardian orchestrating a delicate ballet between fate and destiny.

Rumors began to stir, like ripples on a pond disturbed by an unseen force. Whispers of a mysterious power at play in the city's shadows danced through the air. Grumble's actions, bold and enchanted, drew both ire and curiosity from those who sought to maintain the status quo. And when another goblin dared to challenge Grumble's dominion over Clara, the challenger quickly learned the folly of underestimating a goblin fueled by love.

With every stolen coin and selfless act, Grumble's vision of a new life for Clara began to take shape. He dreamed of a home, adorned with opulence and warmth, where she could find solace and comfort amidst life's chaos.

As Clara's gratitude swelled, so too did a seed of doubt within her heart. She couldn't help but question the source of her newfound fortune, and the mysteries that enshrouded her enigmatic protector.

Then came the moment of truth, when Grumble, with trembling heart, revealed his true identity to Clara. He bared his soul, confessing his love and the lengths he had gone to for her sake. Clara, stunned yet deeply moved, felt a warmth in her heart that illuminated even the darkest corners of doubt.

United by love and a shared dream, Grumble and Clara embarked on a journey to find the perfect sanctuary, a canvas for their future painted with care and joy. With keys in hand, they stepped into a world of luxury and comfort, a testament to the magic and determination that had bound their fates.

Their love story, once whispered in the city's hidden corners, now echoed through its bustling streets. Grumble and Clara's union became a beacon of hope and inspiration, celebrated by friends and allies who had witnessed their extraordinary journey.

And so, the tale of Grumble and Clara unfolded, a saga of magic and love that transcended the boundaries of time and space. Their legacy, etched into the very fabric of the city they called home, would endure through the ages, inspiring generations yet to come.

Chapter 1: The chance encounter

The night air was thick with the scent of rain-soaked pavement as Grumble stood 3'6 inches tall, yearning in the shadows, observing a 5'6 Clara from a distance as he had for what seemed an eternity. Her silhouette was a stark contrast against the city's unforgiving backdrop. Her clothes, tattered and worn, told a story of trials endured.

As Grumble approached, the soft patter of rain mingled with the distant hum of traffic. Clara turned, her eyes meeting Grumble's with a mixture of surprise and wariness. In that moment, time seemed to stand still.

"Are you lost, me-dear?" Grumble's voice, though gruff, held a gentleness that belied his appearance.

Clara's gaze wavered, torn between the stranger before her and the world she knew. Her lips curved into a hesitant smile, revealing the glimmer of a spirit unbroken.

"I... I suppose you could say that," she replied, her voice carrying a hint of vulnerability.

Grumble's heart swelled with empathy. He recognized the strength that dwelled within Clara, a strength forged in the crucible of adversity. It was a strength he had seen in few others.

"Come, let me help," Grumble offered, extending a hand. "There's a warmth and shelter not far from here."

Clara hesitated only for a moment before taking Grumble's hand, allowing herself to be led through the labyrinthine streets. The city's chaos seemed to fade into the background, replaced by a newfound sense of purpose.

As they walked, Grumble couldn't help but steal glances at Clara's face. Her eyes, though weary, held a spark of determination. Her spirit was like a hidden gem, waiting to be unearthed from the depths of hardship.

Finally, they arrived at a small, unassuming building tucked away from the main thoroughfare. Grumble opened the door, revealing a humble yet welcoming interior. Warm light spilled out, dispelling the shadows of the night.

"Welcome, Clara, to your new sanctuary," Grumble declared, his eyes gleaming with a mixture of pride and compassion.

Clara's breath caught in her throat, overcome by the unexpected kindness that had been bestowed upon her. She turned to Grumble, her eyes glistening with gratitude.

"Thank you," she whispered, her voice carrying the weight of a lifetime of struggles.

In that moment, as rain continued its gentle dance outside, Grumble and Clara stood together, two souls brought together by chance. Little did they know that this encounter would be the catalyst for a journey that would change their lives forever.

Grumble watched as Clara stepped tentatively into the welcoming light of the sanctuary. Her eyes scanned the room, taking in the simple comforts that awaited her. A bed with clean linens, a table set with a warm meal, and a small fireplace flickering with dancing flames.

"This is... more than I could have ever hoped for," Clara breathed, her voice filled with wonder.

Grumble nodded, his heart swelling with a mixture of joy and relief. It was a humbling experience, to witness the impact of his small act of kindness on Clara's weary soul.

"You deserve this and more, Clara," Grumble assured her, his gruff voice softening with sincerity. "Rest now, and tomorrow we'll take the first steps toward a brighter future."

As Clara settled into the newfound haven, Grumble slipped back into the night, leaving her to the embrace of warmth and safety. The rain outside had begun to relent, leaving behind a sense of calm in its wake.

In the days that followed, Grumble visited Clara often. They shared stories, dreams, and even moments of quiet companionship. Clara's spirit, once buried beneath the weight of hardship, began to unfurl like a delicate blossom.

As the weeks turned into months, Grumble and Clara forged a bond that went beyond the bounds of mere friendship. They became kindred spirits, each finding solace in the other's presence.

Together, they faced the challenges of the city, navigating its complexities with a newfound determination. Grumble's knowledge of the hidden corners and magical ways proved invaluable, while Clara's resilience and empathy became a beacon of strength.

One evening, under the glow of a full moon, Clara turned to Grumble with a question that had been quietly growing in her heart.

"Grumble, why did you help me that night?" she asked, her eyes searching his.

Grumble met her gaze, the depth of his affection shining through. "Because, Clara, I saw in you a spirit that refused to be extinguished. Your strength inspired me, and I knew I had to do whatever I could to help."

Tears glistened in Clara's eyes, mirroring the emotion that swelled within her chest. She reached out, taking Grumble's weathered hand in hers.

"Then know this, Grumble," she whispered, "you've given me more than shelter and warmth. You've given me hope, and for that, I am forever grateful."

In that moment, beneath the watchful eye of the moon, Grumble and Clara shared a silent understanding. Their hearts beat in rhythm, bound by the unbreakable thread of shared trials and newfound love.

Little did they know that their chance encounter would set in motion a journey filled with magic, love, and the promise of a future brighter than they could have ever imagined.

Chapter 2: Moonlit Promises

As the moon cast its silvery glow upon the city, Grumble and Clara found themselves drawn to the rooftop of their sanctuary. They stood side by side, gazing out at the twinkling lights that adorned the urban landscape.

"This city holds so many stories, doesn't it?" Clara mused, her voice soft with reflection.

Grumble looked up and nodded, his eyes never leaving Clara's face. "And now, it holds ours."

They turned to each other, the weight of their shared journey hanging in the air. In that moment, they knew that their hearts had become entwined in a way that went beyond the realm of mere mortals.

"Clara," Grumble began, his voice steady, "from the first moment I saw you, I knew that our meeting was no mere chance. You are a lady of strength and resilience, and I want to be by your side, always."

Clara's heart fluttered in her chest, her eyes locked onto Grumble's with a mixture of wonder and affection. She took a step closer, closing the gap between them.

"And you, Grumble," she whispered, "you've shown me a kindness that I never dared to hope for. You've breathed life into my spirit, and I can't imagine my days without you."

In that moonlit moment, beneath the vast expanse of the night sky, they made a promise to each other. Their love would be a force that could weather any storm, a shining light of hope that would guide them through whatever challenges the future lay ahead.

As they stood there, their hands entwined, they felt a sense of completeness wash over them. The city's bustling chaos seemed to fade into the background, leaving only the two of them, bound by a love that had blossomed from the most unexpected of beginnings.

From that night forward, Grumble and Clara faced each day with renewed purpose and a shared vision of a future filled with love and possibility. Little did they know that their story would become a legend, whispered among the city's streets, proving the transformative power of love.

In the quiet hours of night, Grumble's small sanctuary was alight with the flickering glow of candles. The room was filled with the scent of ancient herbs and the soft rustle of parchment as Grumble poured over arcane tomes. His heart beat with a fierce determination, fueled by a desire to reshape Clara's world.

With each incantation and carefully woven spell, Grumble's powers surged through him. He summoned shadows to conceal his movements, and whispered ancient words to open paths where there were none. The city's labyrinthine streets became his domain, a realm of endless potential, where his magic wove the threads of fate.

Through clandestine means, Grumble acquired resources to better Clara's life. He transformed discarded treasures into gleaming tokens of fortune, and turned whispers into melodies of promise. The city's underbelly, with its secrets and hidden gems, surrendered to his mastery.

Yet, in his quest to weave this tapestry of change, Grumble garnered the attention of those who dwelled in the shadows, their own ambitions intersecting with his. Whispers of a mysterious force danced through the city's alleys, leaving behind a trail of intrigue and apprehension.

The ire of those he crossed was palpable, their anger a tempest that threatened to engulf Grumble. But he pressed on, fueled by the memory of Clara's eyes, resilient and full of hope.

In the silent watches of night, Grumble's determination remained unyielding. His efforts were guided by a single purpose: to sculpt a future for Clara, one where her spirit would soar unburdened.

As the days turned into weeks, Grumble's enchantments grew in potency and precision. The city, with all its complexities and hidden treasures, yielded to his touch. Each act of magic was a profession to his love for Clara, proclaiming the power that could be wielded in the name of transformation.

Through the weaving of spells and the dance of shadows, Grumble's enchanted ambitions continued to unfold, setting the stage for a destiny that was bound to be nothing short of extraordinary.

Chapter 3: The goblin's secret

The rooftop sanctuary became their refuge, a sacred space where dreams took flight under the moon's watchful eye. Grumble and Clara, bound by their shared vision, held fast to one another, drawing strength from the love that pulsed between them.

As the city below continued its relentless dance, Grumble's enchantments grew in complexity and power. Each precious artifact acquired, each whispered spell, was a testament to his unwavering devotion to Clara. It was as if the very essence of the city responded to his touch, unfurling its hidden wonders like petals kissed by the morning sun.

Yet, amid their fervent pursuit of a better future, the shadows that lurked in the city's depths stirred with restless energy. Whispers of an ancient, enigmatic force threaded through the alleys, weaving an ominous counterpoint to Grumble's own magic. It was a force he could not afford to ignore, for it threatened not only their ambitions, but the very sanctuary they had forged together.

One evening, with the moon casting a silvery glow upon them, Grumble turned to Clara, his eyes a mix of determination and concern. "Clara, there's something you must know. The path I tread, the magic I wield... it is not without peril. There are ancient, powerful forces in this city that may seek to thwart our endeavors."

Clara met his gaze, her eyes unwavering in their trust. "Grumble, we face this together. Whatever challenges arise, we will meet them as we always have - united."

Her words were a source of strength for Grumble, a reminder that their love was an unbreakable bond. With Clara by his side, he felt an unyielding resolve, a belief that together, they could conquer any obstacle.

Beneath the moon's benevolent gaze, they made a solemn pact. They would press forward, undaunted by the shadows that loomed, their love was the most warm and magical light that brought them through the darkness of each night.

As days turned to nights, and nights to weeks, Grumble's magic wove a tapestry of change that stretched across the city. Its once formidable obstacles began to yield, revealing hidden treasures and opportunities. Clara's spirit, kindled by their shared journey, radiated a brilliance that lit the path before them.

Their rooftop sanctuary bore witness to their aspirations, their vulnerabilities, and their unshakeable love. Together, they stood as a force to be reckoned with, a testament to the profound transformation that love, in its purest form, could bring about.

As the nights passed, Clara remained unaware of the magical efforts woven to better her life. Grumble, shrouded in secrecy, watched over her from the shadows, orchestrating the dance between fate and destiny.

In the quiet hours of the night, when the city slumbered and dreams stirred in the hearts of its inhabitants, Grumble would set forth on his clandestine missions. Cloaked in the night's embrace, he moved with the grace of a phantom, leaving no trace of his presence.

His magic, honed through years of devotion to Clara's cause, became an extension of himself. He wove spells of prosperity, coaxing forgotten treasures to gleam once more. He whispered incantations of protection, ensuring Clara's safety in a world that often seemed unyielding.

Clara, meanwhile, navigated the waking world with a growing sense of wonder and gratitude. The changes that bloomed around her were like ripples in a pond, emanating from a source she could not fathom. She felt a newfound strength within herself, a resilience that seemed to draw strength from the very air around her.

Little did she suspect the goblin, the quiet guardian who toiled in the shadows, pouring his heart and magic into every endeavor. The rooftop sanctuary, their shared haven, remained a sacred space where their hearts intertwined, their souls dancing in silent harmony.

Yet, as the city's heartbeat pulsed on, Grumble sensed the looming presence of the enigmatic force. It was a palpable tension, a gathering storm on the horizon. He knew that their sanctuary, their love, could not remain hidden forever.

One night, as the stars painted patterns across the sky, Grumble returned to the rooftop, his eyes reflecting the weight of his secret. Clara turned to him, her gaze filled with trust and affection.

"Grumble," she said softly, "there's something I've been meaning to tell you. I feel a change within me, as if the very city breathes with a new rhythm. It's as if... magic courses through its veins."

Grumble met her gaze, a mixture of pride and trepidation in his eyes. "Clara, my dear, you are perceptive. The city has indeed responded to the love and hope that reside within you."

He hesitated for a moment, then continued, his voice tinged with solemnity. "But we must also be vigilant, for there are forces that would seek to unravel what we've built."

Clara nodded, her spirit undaunted. "Whatever comes our way, Grumble, we face it together."

And so, beneath the ever-watchful stars, they stood united, ready to confront the mysteries and challenges that awaited them. Grumble's secret remained safe, but the echoes of destiny whispered through the city, heralding a future that held both promise and peril.

In their sanctuary atop the world, Grumble and Clara found solace in each other's arms. The moon, their silent witness, bathed them in its tender light, as if bestowing its blessing upon their love.

As the nights passed, Grumble's enchantments took on a life of their own, interweaving with the very fabric of the city. The streets seemed to whisper their approval, and the forgotten corners yielded their secrets willingly. It was as if the city itself recognized the love that Grumble and Clara shared, and responded in kind.

Yet, beneath the surface of their burgeoning paradise, the shadows stirred with an uneasy energy. The enigmatic force, like a storm gathering strength, loomed ever closer. Grumble knew that their sanctuary, though powerful, was not impervious to the currents of fate.

One night, as the stars blinked in quiet contemplation, Grumble and Clara stood together on their rooftop refuge. Clara's eyes shone with an inner light, her soul attuned to the subtle shifts around her.

"Grumble," she began, her voice a melodic symphony in the night, "I feel it too. The city, it's alive with something... extraordinary."

Grumble's heart swelled with a mixture of pride and concern. "Clara, you have a gift for seeing the magic that others overlook. The love you carry within you has touched this city in ways we may never fully understand."

He took a breath, his eyes fixed on Clara's. "But we must also be vigilant. There are ancient forces at play, and they may not view our endeavors with the same benevolence."

Clara's gaze held steady, her determination unwavering. "Then we face them together, Grumble. With our love as our shield, we will overcome whatever comes our way."

With those words, they sealed their pact beneath the endless expanse of stars. The city's heartbeat echoed around them, a steady rhythm to which their love danced in time.

As days turned to nights and nights to weeks, Grumble's magic wove its intricate tapestry. Clara, guided by her intuition, discovered newfound strengths within herself. Their sanctuary became a haven not only for them, but for the city's hidden wonders and forgotten dreams.

And still, Grumble's secret remained veiled in the quiet of night, a tale known only to the moon and the stars. Destiny, like a river's current, flowed ever onward, carrying with it the promise of a future woven from love's enduring thread.

In the heart of their sanctuary, Grumble and Clara's love blossomed, illuminated by the moon's gentle embrace. Their rooftop refuge became a sacred space, a haven where dreams took flight, and where two souls, bound by an unbreakable bond, found solace.

As the nights unfurled, Grumble's enchantments gained a life of their own, weaving themselves into the very essence of the city. The streets, once impassive, now seemed to pulse with a quiet approval. Forgotten corners willingly offered up their secrets, as if acknowledging the love that Grumble and Clara held.

Yet, beneath the surface of their idyllic haven, the shadows stirred with an energy both restless and foreboding. The enigmatic force, like a tempest on the horizon, drew nearer. Grumble understood that their sanctuary, though powerful, was not impervious to the ebbs and flows of destiny.

One night, as the stars blinked in quiet contemplation, Grumble and Clara stood together on their rooftop sanctuary. Clara's eyes shone with an inner light, her spirit attuned to the subtle shifts around her.

"Grumble," she began, her voice a melody that seemed to harmonize with the night itself, "I sense it too. The city, it's alive with something... extraordinary."

Grumble's heart swelled with a mixture of pride and concern. "Clara, you possess a rare gift for perceiving the magic that often eludes others. The love you carry within you has woven itself into the very fabric of this city, creating ripples that may shape its destiny in ways we can scarcely imagine."

He paused, his gaze locked darkly onto Clara's. "Yet, may I remind you yet again, we must always be vigilant. There are ancient forces at work, and they will not regard our endeavors with the same benevolence."

Clara's gaze remained steady, her resolve unyielding. "Then we face them together, Grumble. With our love as our powerful sheild, we shall overcome whatever challenges may come our way to the absolute"

With those words, they sealed their pact even tighter beneath the celestial canopy of stars. The city's heartbeat echoed with an ache around them, a steady rhythm that seemed to synchronize with the beating of their own hearts.

As neverending days melted into countless nights and into many following weeks, Grumble's magic continued still to weave its intricate tapestry. Clara, guided by her intuition, discovered wellsprings of strength within herself. Their sanctuary transformed into a forever-haven not just for them, but for the city's hidden wonders and forgotten dreams.

And yet, Grumble's secret stil remained sheltered in the cocoon of night, a story known only to the moon and the stars. Destiny flowed on in Grumble's favor, an eternal river, carrying with it the promise of a future fashioned from the very same enduring thread of love.

Chapter 4: Whispers of Destiny

The city, with its labyrinthine streets and towering spires, continued its ceaseless song. Grumble and Clara, intertwined in their love, faced each day with a sense of purpose that resonated with the very heartbeat of the metropolis.

Grumble's enchantments had become a part of the city's essence, threading through its stones and alleys. Whispers of gratitude seemed to drift on the wind, carried by unseen hands. The forgotten corners, once shrouded in shadows, now basked in a newfound light.

Yet, beneath the surface, the enigmatic force loomed ever nearer. Grumble felt it like a distant thunder, a storm gathering strength. He was convinced that their sanctuary, though fortified by love, sadly could not remain concealed forever.

One night, as the moon hung low, Grumble and Clara stood together on their rooftop haven. Clara's eyes held a depth of understanding, her spirit attuned to the city's pulse.

"Grumble," she said, her voice steady, "the city feels alive, as though it's part of a grand tapestry, woven with threads of magic and love."

Grumble's heart swelled with pride, tempered by caution. "Clara, you have a poet's soul and a seer's eyes. The magic we've stirred in this city flows like a river through its veins."

He looked at her, his eyes filled with admiration. "But we must also remember, there are ancient powers at play. They may not share our vision for the city's future."

Clara's gaze remained resolute. "Then we shall face them together, Grumble. Our love is a force that can weather any storm."

And so, beneath the silent watch of the moon, they reaffirmed their pledge. The city seemed to echo their resolve, its heartbeat a steady loud drumming.

Days turned into nights, and nights into weeks. Grumble's enchantments continued on and on to shape the city, while Clara's own spirit blossomed. Their sanctuary, once hidden, now stood as an exposed beacon of hope and transformation.

Grumble's secret remained nestled in the night's embrace. The moon and stars, the silent witnesses to their tale, held the knowledge close.

Destiny flowed on, its currents weaving through the city's streets. Grumble and Clara, bound by love and purpose, stood ready to face whatever whispered challenges awaited them, knowing that together, they were dark forces not to be reckoned with.

The city, with its tangled streets and towering spires, continued its ceaseless song. Grumble and Clara, intertwined in their love, faced each day with a sense of purpose that resonated with the very heartbeat of their metropolis.

Grumble's enchantments had become a part of the city's essence, threading through its stones and alleys. Whispers of gratitude seemed to drift on the wind, carried by unseen hands. The forgotten corners, once long ago shrouded in shadows, now basked in a constant magic light.

Yet, beneath the surface, the enigmatic force loomed ever nearer. Grumble felt it like a distant thunder, a storm gathering strength. He knew that their sanctuary, though fortified by love, could not remain concealed forever.

One night, as the moon hung low, Grumble and Clara stood together on their rooftop haven. Clara's eyes held a depth of understanding, her spirit attuned to the city's pulse.

"Grumble," she said, her voice steady, "the city feels alive, as though it's part of a grand tapestry, woven with threads of magic and love."

He looked at her, his eyes filled with his secret. "But we must also remember, there are ancient powers at play. They can not share *our* vision for the city's future."

Clara's gaze remained resolute. "Then we shall face them together, Grumble. Our love is a force that can weather any storm."

And so, beneath the silent watch of the moon, they yet again reaffirmed their pledge. The city did echo their resolve, its heartbeat a steady drumming even louder.

Grumble's secret remained. The moon and stars, the silent witnesses to the tale, held the knowledge close.

Destiny flowed on, its currents weaving through the city's streets. Grumble and Clara, bound by love and purpose, stood ready.

Beneath the glittering facade of the city's grandeur, a current of unease flowed through its underbelly. Rumors spread like wildfire, carried on hushed voices and exchanged glances. There was talk of a force, something powerful and unseen, that moved through the city's veins, leaving ripples in its wake.

Grumble's actions did not go unnoticed. His enchantments, once hidden in the shadows, now brazenly danced through the streets, leaving behind a trail of change. For others, it was a disruption, a challenge to the established order.

In the heart of the city's darkness, where secrets whispered through narrow alleyways, discontent brewed. Figures cloaked in shadows gathered, their murmurs filled with a mixture of anger and curiosity. They sought to unearth the truth behind the transformation that was sweeping through the city.

One fateful night, as the moon hung low, a challenger emerged from the depths of the underbelly. Another goblin, eyes gleaming with a mixture of envy and lust, sought to challenge Grumble and steal Clara away.

The confrontation was swift and fierce. Grumble, with a heart fueled by love and determination, faced the intruder with a steely resolve. Shadows coalesced around him, his magic like a deadly hammer a formidable force. The clash echoed through the narrow alley, the air charged with electricity.

Clara, though startled by the sudden turn of events, stood her ground, her spirit unwavering. She watched with a mixture of awe and concern as blood spill onto the streets. Grumble, with a deftness born of experience, subdued the challenger.

In the end, the defeated goblin slunk back into the shadows, his aspirations crushed by Grumble's unwavering devotion. Clara, her heart pounding, rushed to Grumble's side, her eyes filled with gratitude and concern.

"You... you saved me," she whispered, her voice trembling with emotion.

Grumble, though wearied by the encounter, met Clara's gaze with a fierce determination. "I will always protect you, Clara. Our love is a force that cannot be broken." as he followed the enemy into the shadows.

And so, in the aftermath of the confrontation, whispers of discontent continued to ripple through the city's underbelly. Grumble's actions had not only incited curiosity but had also drawn the ire of those who sought to maintain the status quo. The conquered goblin now a missing person as a search begun.

Grumble was undeterred. With Clara by his side, he would face whatever challenges came their way. The city, with all its complexities and hidden wonders, was a tapestry waiting to be woven, and Grumble was determined to leave his mark upon it.

The defeated challenger's disappearance left the narrow alley in profound silence, saved for the distant echoes of the city's pulse. Clara's eyes remained locked onto Grumble's, a profound mixture of awe and gratitude in her gaze.

"You... you saved me," she breathed, her voice tinged with emotion.

Grumble's weariness was eclipsed by the fire that still burned in his eyes. "I will always protect you, my Clara. Our love is a force that cannot be broken."

They stood there, two souls bound by an unbreakable bond, in the heart of the city's clandestine labyrinth. The moon watched over them, its silver glow casting a tranquil aura upon the scene.

As the days pressed on, the whispers of discontent persisted, a symphony of voices that danced through the city's hidden alcoves. Grumble's actions, both magical and bold, continued to be a source of fascination and consternation.

Yet, he pressed forward, undeterred by the shadows that clung to the city's edges. With Clara by his side, he knew that their love was a beacon that could guide them through any storm.

The city, with all its complexities and hidden wonders, awaited their touch. Grumble was determined to leave his mark, to weave a tapestry of change that would be felt for generations to come.

And so, hand in hand, they ventured forth, ready to face whatever challenges destiny had in store. For in the heart of the city's underbelly, amidst whispers of discontent, Grumble and Clara's love shone brighter than ever in their unbreakable bonds of the heart.

Chapter 5: Dreams of a New Home

In the quiet moments between spells and shadows, Grumble allowed himself to dream. He envisioned a future for Clara, one that sparkled with the promise of comfort and contentment. Each stolen coin and act of generosity was a step towards realizing that vision.

In the heart of the city, where the rhythm of life pulsed strongest, Grumble sought out the finest craftsmen and artisans. He commissioned works of art that would adorn the walls of their future home, each piece a testament to the beauty he saw in Clara's spirit.

He imagined rooms bathed in soft hues, where the gentle glow of candles would chase away the night's shadows. Plush fabrics and sumptuous furnishings would invite Clara to sink into a world of comfort, a sanctuary away from the chaos of the city.

The garden, Grumble decided, would be a place of magic in itself. He envisioned vibrant blooms and winding paths, where Clara could lose herself in nature's embrace. It would be a haven of serenity, a place where dreams could take root and flourish.

As the days turned into weeks, Grumble's efforts bore fruit. The city's secrets yielded treasures that glittered like stars, each one a promise of the life he envisioned for Clara.

One evening, beneath the glow of the moon, Grumble turned to Clara, his eyes shining with anticipation. "Clara, there's something I've been dreaming of. A home for us, a place where you can find peace and joy."

Clara's eyes widened in wonder, touched by Grumble's words. "A home? Oh, Grumble, I could never have imagined..."

Grumble took her hand, his heart full. "You deserve nothing less, Clara. With each act of magic, with every stolen coin, I've been building towards this dream. A place where our love will shine brighter than ever."

And so, with a shared vision in their hearts, Grumble and Clara looked to the future. The city's whispers and shadows could not dim the light of their dreams. Together, they would forge a new home, a haven where their love would bloom, a testament to the power of dreams woven with love's gentle touch.

Under the watchful gaze of the moon, Grumble's dream took shape. The finest craftsmen and artisans were summoned, their talents guided by Grumble's vision. Each stroke of a brush, each chisel's careful touch, brought life to the home he had imagined.

The walls, once barren, now held the soul of their sanctuary. Paintings and tapestries depicted scenes of beauty and wonder, capturing the essence of Clara's spirit. Every room, from the grand hall to the coziest nook, bore the mark of Grumble's devotion.

Candles flickered in sconces, their warm light dancing across the walls. The air held the scent of lavender and cedar, a soothing balm for the soul. Plush cushions adorned the furniture, inviting Clara to rest and find solace in their haven.

The garden, once a neglected patch of earth, now thrived with vibrant blooms. Grumble's magic wove through the soil, coaxing life from every seed. Winding paths led to hidden alcoves, where Clara could read, dream, and find respite in the embrace of nature.

As the final brushstrokes were laid, as the last seedling found its place, Grumble and Clara stood hand in hand, their hearts filled with awe. The home that had existed only in their dreams now stood before them, a testament to the power of love's imagination.

Clara's eyes shone with unshed tears of gratitude. "Grumble, this is more than I could have ever imagined. It's a place where our love will live and breathe."

Grumble's voice was filled with emotion. "It's a reflection of the light you've brought into my life, Clara. Every corner, every brushstroke, is a testament to the beauty you've shown me."

And so, in their newly created haven, Grumble and Clara's love found a home. The city's whispers of discontent were drowned out by the laughter and warmth that echoed through their halls. Together, they had forged a sanctuary, a place where dreams took root and flourished, a testament to the power of love and the magic it could weave.

As the first light of dawn painted the sky with soft hues of pink and gold, Grumble and Clara stepped over the threshold of their new home. The air seemed to hold its breath, as if in reverence for the love that now dwelled within these walls.

The grand hall welcomed them with open arms, its walls adorned with tapestries that told the story of their journey. Each thread seemed to shimmer with a life of its own, weaving a tale of magic and devotion. Clara's fingers brushed against the fabric, tracing the familiar contours of their shared adventures.

They moved from room to room, each one revealing its own unique charm. The cozy nook by the window, where Clara could lose herself in a book and Grumble could watch over her with a contented heart. The kitchen, where the aroma of freshly baked bread mingled with the scent of herbs from the garden, promising warmth and nourishment.

In the garden, blooms greeted them with vibrant colors, a chorus of life that seemed to dance in the morning breeze. Clara's laughter filled the air as she discovered hidden alcoves and secret corners, each one a testament to Grumble's boundless love.

As the day unfolded, Grumble and Clara settled into their new home, their hearts brimming with gratitude and wonder. Every corner held a memory, every detail a reflection of the love that had built it.

In the quiet moments, when the world outside seemed to fade away, they stood together in the heart of their sanctuary. Clara turned to Grumble, her eyes sparkling with unspoken emotions. "Grumble, this is more than I could have ever dreamed. It's a symphony of love, woven into every brick and blossom."

Grumble's gaze never wavered from Clara's. "It's a reflection of the love that has blossomed between us, Clara. This home is a testament to the magic we've created together."

And so, in the heart of their sanctuary, Grumble and Clara's love found its truest expression. The city's whispers of discontent were but distant echoes, drowned out by the harmony that resonated within these walls.

As the sun dipped below the horizon, casting the world in shades of twilight, Grumble and Clara stood together, hand in hand. Their dreams had taken root, their love had found a home, and their future stretched before them, a blank canvas waiting to be filled with the colors of their shared adventures.

In the embrace of their new home, Grumble and Clara discovered a haven where their love could flourish, each moment an echo of their intertwined souls. As the sun dipped below the horizon, they stood in the tranquil courtyard, hand in hand, its stone paths illuminated by the warm glow of lanterns.

The night sky unfurled above them, a canvas painted with stars, as if to bless their journey forward. Clara turned to Grumble, her eyes reflecting the brilliance of the heavens.

"Grumble," she began, her voice a soft melody, "this home, it's a testament to the love that has woven us together. Every corner, every detail, it speaks of our shared journey."

Grumble's heart swelled with a profound tenderness. "Clara, it is a reflection of the light you've brought into my life. Each brick, each bloom, is a manifestation of the beauty you've shown me."

In that moment, beneath the tapestry of the night, they knew that their love story was woven into the very fabric of their home. It was a sanctuary where dreams would continue to unfold, where each day would be a testament to the power of their shared love.

As they turned to re-enter their haven, a soft breeze rustled the leaves, as if whispering its approval. The night held a promise of adventures yet to be written, of chapters waiting to unfold.

And so, Grumble and Clara stepped forward, ready to embrace the future that awaited them. Their hearts beat in time with the rhythm of the city, a reminder that their story was but one verse in the symphony of life.

As the door closed behind them, the night held its breath, waiting to see what new wonders would emerge from the love that now dwelled within those walls.

Inside the warmth of their sanctuary, Grumble and Clara stood together, their hearts echoing the quiet serenade of the night. The soft glow of lanterns cast dancing shadows, painting their surroundings with an ethereal beauty.

Clara turned to Grumble, her eyes holding the same starlit wonder that adorned the sky. "Grumble," she whispered, "this home feels like a dream woven from our hearts. It's a place where our love has found its truest form."

Grumble's voice, gentle as a breeze through the leaves, replied, "Clara, this home is a testament to the magic that we share. Every stone, every petal, is a reflection of the love that has transformed our lives."

As they moved through the rooms, the air seemed to shimmer with enchantment, as if the very walls absorbed the essence of their love. Each step was a promise, each breath an affirmation of the life they would build together.

In the quiet of their bedroom, Clara stood by the window, the moonlight casting a silvery glow on her face. Grumble approached, his hand finding hers with a tenderness that spoke volumes. Together, they gazed out at the city, its heart pulsing in time with theirs.

"Clara," Grumble murmured, "this city, our home, it holds a future as boundless as the stars. With you by my side, I know that we can overcome any challenge, face any unknown."

Clara turned to him, her eyes reflecting the moon's gentle light. "Grumble, our love has already overcome so much. Together, there's nothing we can't achieve."

In that moment, their hearts beat in harmonious rhythm, a promise of adventures yet to be written, of chapters waiting to unfold. With every sunrise, they would wake to a world filled with possibilities, knowing that their love was the foundation upon which their dreams would flourish.

As they settled into their bed, their hands still entwined, the night held its breath, cradling them in its tender embrace. The stars above seemed to wink in silent approval, as if blessing the love story that had found its home within those walls.

And so, Grumble and Clara drifted into dreams, their hearts entwined, their souls dancing in the quiet symphony of the night.

Chapter 6: Shadows of Doubt

In the quiet moments of reflection, Clara found herself tracing the threads of her new life, each strand woven with the magic and kindness that Grumble had bestowed upon her. The home they shared was a sanctuary, a haven where their love bloomed like the vibrant blooms in their garden. Yet, beneath the surface of her gratitude, a seed of doubt took root.

As Clara moved through the rooms, admiring the tapestries and art that adorned the walls, she couldn't help but wonder about the enigmatic force that seemed to breathe life into their sanctuary. The question lingered like a whisper in the back of her mind, growing with each passing day.

One evening, as the moon bathed their home in a soft, silvery light, Clara turned to Grumble, her eyes filled with a mix of curiosity and concern. "Grumble, there's something I've been meaning to ask. All of this... this beautiful home, the magic that surrounds us... where does it come from?"

Grumble met her gaze, his eyes reflecting the constellations above. "Clara, my dear, it comes from a place of love and a desire to see you thrive. Every act of magic, every stolen coin, is a testament to the dreams we share."

Clara's heart swelled with affection for the goblin who had become her protector and confidante. Yet, the seed of doubt still lingered, its tendrils weaving through her thoughts.

"But Grumble," she ventured, "there are whispers in the city, shadows of doubt. Some wonder about the source of our good fortune, and I find myself wondering too."

Grumble's expression softened, and he took Clara's hands in his. "Clara, I understand your concern. The world can be filled with skepticism and mistrust. But know this: every enchantment, every treasure, is borne from a place of pure intent. It is a testament to the love that binds us, and to the dreams we hold for our future."

Clara looked into Grumble's eyes, finding solace in his unwavering gaze. In that moment, she chose to trust in the love that had blossomed between them. The shadows of doubt, though present, were no match for the light they shared.

And so, as the moon continued its gentle watch over their home, Clara and Grumble stood united, their hearts entwined. The seed of doubt, once nestled in Clara's heart, began to fade, replaced by a blossoming trust in the magic that had woven their lives together. Together, they would face whatever mysteries the future held, knowing that their love would light the way.

In the days that followed, Clara allowed herself to bask in the warmth of their shared love, embracing the sanctuary they had built together. Grumble's words echoed in her heart, a soothing balm to the seed of doubt that had taken root.

As the sun bathed their home in golden hues, Clara found comfort in the familiar cadence of their days. She reveled in the simple joys—the whispered conversations in the garden, the shared laughter over meals, and the stolen glances that spoke volumes.

Grumble, ever attuned to Clara's heart, watched over her with a tenderness that spoke of a love deeper than words. He knew the shadows of doubt still lingered, and he vowed to dispel them with the unwavering light of his devotion.

One evening, beneath the canvas of a star-strewn sky, Grumble led Clara to the garden. The blooms nodded in agreement, as if privy to the weight of Clara's thoughts.

"Clara," Grumble began, his voice a gentle melody in the night, "I see the questions that linger in your eyes. Know this, my dearest: every act of magic, every stolen coin, is a testament to the dreams we hold. It is born of a love that defies the boundaries of this world."

Clara met his gaze, her heart stirred by the sincerity in his words. "Grumble, you've given me a life filled with wonder and love. I want to trust in the magic you've woven for us."

Grumble's eyes sparkled with gratitude, and he took Clara's hand, his touch a reassurance of the unbreakable bond they shared. "Clara, together, we are bound by a love that transcends doubt and fear. Our sanctuary is a testament to the power of that love."

In that moment, Clara felt a profound sense of peace settle within her. The seed of doubt, once a thorn in her heart, had withered and faded, replaced by a resolute trust in the magic that had brought them together.

And so, beneath the watchful gaze of the stars, Clara and Grumble stood united, their hearts entwined by a love that had overcome shadows of doubt. As they turned to re-enter their sanctuary, Clara knew that their journey, guided by love's unwavering light, would lead them to even greater wonders.

Under the embrace of the starlit heavens, Clara and Grumble stepped back into their sanctuary. The night seemed to hold its breath, as if in reverence for the strength of their love.

In the days that followed, Clara's heart found a newfound serenity. The whispers of doubt had been replaced by an unyielding trust in the magic that bound them. She reveled in the moments, both grand and intimate, that painted the canvas of their shared life.

The garden, once a place of blooms and contemplation, now held an even deeper significance. It was a living testament to the power of trust and the beauty that blossomed from it. Clara would often lose herself among the vibrant colors, finding solace in the gentle embrace of nature.

As the seasons danced on, their sanctuary became a haven not only for Clara and Grumble but for those who felt the undeniable magic that dwelled within. The city, once shrouded in whispers of doubt, now bore witness to a love that defied boundaries.

One evening, as the sun dipped below the horizon, Clara stood with Grumble in the heart of their sanctuary. She turned to him, her eyes reflecting the quiet wisdom that had grown within her.

"Grumble," she began, her voice a gentle affirmation, "our love has transformed not only our lives but also this city. It's a testament to the power of trust and the magic that weaves through our existence."

Grumble's heart swelled with pride and affection for the woman who had become his partner in every sense of the word. "Clara, you are the truest magic in my life. Together, we've forged a sanctuary where love reigns supreme."

And so, as the days turned into nights, and nights into dreams, Clara and Grumble's sanctuary stood as a beacon of hope and trust in the heart of the city. The shadows of doubt had long since faded, replaced by the brilliant light of a love that had overcome all obstacles.

Their journey, guided by trust, had unfurled in ways they could have never imagined. And as they stood hand in hand, beneath the ever-watchful stars, they knew that their love's story was destined to continue, painting new chapters on the canvas of their shared existence.

Chapter 7: The Goblin's Sacrifice

The city's heartbeat pulsed with an undercurrent of tension, as if sensing the impending shift in destiny. Grumble, his heart heavy with the weight of secrets, knew that the time had come to reveal the truth to Clara.

One evening, as the moon cast its silvery glow over their sanctuary, Grumble led Clara to their favorite corner of the garden. The blooms whispered their approval, as if aware of the momentousness of the occasion.

Clara turned to Grumble, her eyes filled with trust and affection. "Grumble, you seem... different tonight. Is everything alright?"

Grumble took a deep breath, his gaze unwavering. "Clara, there's something I must confess. It's a truth I've held close, out of fear that it might change the way you see me."

Clara's brow furrowed in concern. "Grumble, you can tell me anything. We face the unknown together, remember?"

Grumble nodded, his heart pounding with a mixture of apprehension and determination. "Clara, my dearest, I am not as I appear. I am a goblin, bound by magic and fate. I chose this form to watch over you, to protect and cherish you from the shadows."

Clara's eyes widened in astonishment, her gaze locked onto Grumble's. "A goblin? But... how is this possible?"

Grumble continued, his voice filled with sincerity. He spoke of his love for Clara, of the lengths he had gone to in order to ensure her safety and happiness. He confessed the enchantments, the stolen coins, and the dreams he had woven for her.

Clara listened, her heart a symphony of emotions. As the truth unfurled, she felt a warmth enveloping her, a sensation she had never known. It was a love that transcended the boundaries of the ordinary, a love that had traveled through time and form to find her.

Tears glistened in Clara's eyes as she reached out to Grumble, her hand finding his. "Grumble, your sacrifice, your love... it's more than I could have ever imagined. You've shown me a depth of devotion that knows no bounds."

Grumble's eyes sparkled with gratitude and relief. "Clara, you are the heart of my existence. With you, I have found a purpose and a love that spans beyond the limits of this world."

And so, beneath the moon's benevolent gaze, Clara and Grumble stood united, their souls entwined in a love that defied convention. The goblin's sacrifice, born of love's boundless well, had illuminated their path, painting a future that held the promise of endless wonders.

With each passing day, Clara and Grumble's love story continued to unfold, a tale woven with threads of magic, devotion, and boundless wonder. Their sanctuary stood as a beacon, a testament to the enduring power of love that defied all odds.

As the city's seasons transitioned, painting vibrant hues across the landscape, Clara and Grumble embraced the changing tides of their lives. Together, they discovered new wonders and faced every challenge with a unity that seemed to draw strength from their shared truth.

Their bond, forged through the crucible of revelation, only deepened with time. Clara marveled at the richness Grumble had brought into her life, seeing beyond the surface to the heart of the goblin who had captured her love.

Grumble, in turn, cherished every moment he spent with Clara, finding in her an endless source of inspiration and a beacon of light that dispelled the shadows of his past. Together, they danced through life, hand in hand, unafraid of whatever mysteries awaited them.

One evening, as they stood on their rooftop refuge, the moon and stars bearing witness to their journey, Clara turned to Grumble. "You know, Grumble, I used to believe that love was bound by the rules of the world. But with you, I've learned that love is boundless. It reaches beyond time and form."

Grumble's eyes shimmered with affection. "Clara, you are the embodiment of that boundless love. With you, I've come to understand that our souls are capable of miracles."

As the years passed, their sanctuary evolved, mirroring the growth of their love. New tapestries wove themselves into the walls, capturing the ever-unfolding chapters of their shared story. The garden, once vibrant, now held a serenity that spoke of a love that had stood the test of time.

And so, as the moon and stars continued their timeless dance, Clara and Grumble found solace in the knowledge that their love was a force that defied all boundaries. Together, they faced the future with hearts open to endless wonders, knowing that their journey was one for the ages, a testament to the boundless power of love's embrace.

Chapter 8: A Promise Fulfilled

United by love and a shared dream, Grumble and Clara stood on the precipice of a new adventure. The vision of their perfect home shimmered before them, a beacon of promise waiting to be realized.

Hand in hand, they ventured forth into the world, eager to find the canvas upon which they would paint their future. Through bustling markets and quaint villages, they sought the elements that would bring their dream to life.

Clara's eyes sparkled with wonder as she explored each possibility, her heart in sync with Grumble's. They reveled in the joy of discovery, finding treasures in unexpected places. Each piece they chose held a special significance, a reflection of the love that bound them.

In the heart of an ancient forest, they discovered the perfect timber for their home, its grain telling tales of ages long past. They journeyed to a distant town, where skilled artisans crafted windows that would invite the sun's golden embrace.

Every detail was chosen with care, from the tiles that would grace their kitchen to the tapestries that would adorn their walls. Each selection was a promise, a pledge to the life they would build together.

As they ventured back to their sanctuary, laden with the fruits of their journey, Grumble and Clara's hearts swelled with anticipation. Their dream was taking shape, a testament to the power of shared vision and boundless love.

With every stroke of a brush, with every nail driven into place, their home emerged from the raw materials of the world. It was a labor of love, a testament to their unwavering commitment to one another.

And then, one golden afternoon, as the final touches were laid, Clara and Grumble stood back to admire their creation. Their home, bathed in the warm glow of the setting sun, stood as a living testament to their shared journey.

The walls echoed with the laughter that had filled the air during their labor, and the rooms seemed to breathe with the promise of a thousand tomorrows. Clara and Grumble's eyes met, shimmering with pride and gratitude. They had taken a vision and, through boundless love and unwavering determination, turned it into reality.

As the days turned into years, their home became a sanctuary not just for them, but for all who entered its welcoming embrace. Friends gathered around the hearth, and children's laughter danced through the halls. Every corner held a memory, every room a story.

Through seasons of joy and moments of challenge, Grumble and Clara stood united, their love growing deeper with each passing day. Their home was a living testament to the power of dreams realized, of shared vision, and of the strength that comes from facing life's challenges hand in hand.

And so, as the sun set on each day, casting a warm golden glow over their haven, Clara and Grumble would often stand together, gazing out at the world they had created. United by love and a shared dream, they knew that their adventure was ongoing, that there were still new chapters waiting to be written.

With hearts full of gratitude, they looked forward to whatever the future held, knowing that as long as they faced it together, their story would continue to be one of beauty, of love, and of a dream fulfilled.

As the years passed, the landscape around their home changed, mirroring the transformations within. The once-ancient forest now stood as a sentinel of their enduring love, its branches reaching towards the sky in silent salute. Flowers, carefully planted by Clara's hand, painted the surroundings with vibrant hues, a testament to the life that flourished in their care.

Their days were marked by the rhythm of shared routines and the sweet surprises that life unfurled. Grumble, with his strong hands and gentle heart, tended to the garden, coaxing life from the earth. Clara, with her keen eye for beauty and grace, filled their home with art and warmth. Together, they wove a tapestry of love and purpose, each day adding a new thread to the intricate design.

As the children grew, the halls echoed with the pitter-patter of little feet, and the rooms echoed with their laughter. Grumble and Clara reveled in their roles as parents, passing down the lessons of love, perseverance, and the joy of dreaming big. They watched with pride as their children, guided by the same values that had built their home, ventured forth into the world to create their own stories.

Through the ebb and flow of life's seasons, Clara and Grumble's love remained steadfast. They weathered storms, both literal and metaphorical, finding strength in their unity. Their home, once a dream on the precipice, now stood as a beacon of hope for all who crossed its threshold.

As they aged, they would often steal quiet moments on the porch, hands entwined, watching the sun paint the sky in hues of gold and pink. They marveled at the legacy they had built, not just in the walls that surrounded them, but in the hearts they had touched along the way.

And when the time came to pass the torch to the next generation, Clara and Grumble did so with grace, knowing that the love and dreams they had nurtured would continue to flourish in the hands of those they loved most.

Their story, a testament to love's enduring power, would echo through the generations, a reminder that dreams, when nurtured with love and boundless determination, have the power to shape not only homes, but the very essence of life itself.

As Clara and Grumble's children took up the mantle of stewardship, the old house continued to thrive, embracing new chapters and evolving with the times. Each generation brought their own touch, their own dreams, weaving them into the fabric of the family's legacy.

The once-ancient forest, now even older, watched over the passing of seasons and the comings and goings of the family it had come to know so well. The flowers, though tended by different hands, still burst forth in riotous color, a testament to the enduring love that had first planted them.

The tapestry of love and purpose that Clara and Grumble had woven continued to grow, each thread representing a member of the expanding family. From lively family gatherings to quiet moments of reflection, the house held the memories of countless moments, etched into its very foundation.

As the years pressed on, the porch became a place of gathering for not just Clara and Grumble, but for their children and grandchildren. It was a space where stories were shared, laughter rang out, and the wisdom of generations was passed down.

The legacy of Clara and Grumble, and the dream they had turned into reality, was a living, breathing entity. It was in the stories told around the fireplace, in the echoes of footsteps on the worn wooden floors, and in the way the sun still painted the sky in hues of gold and pink, just as it always had.

And so, as Clara and Grumble looked back on a life well-lived, they knew that their story was just one chapter in a much larger tale. The home they had built, the dreams they had nurtured, and the love they had shared would continue to shape the lives of generations yet to come.

As the sun set one final time, casting its warm glow over their beloved haven, Clara and Grumble held hands, their hearts full of gratitude for the journey they had taken together. Their story, a testament to the enduring power of love and dreams, would live on in the hearts and homes of their descendants, forever echoing through the ages.

Chapter 9: A New Beginning

With the keys to their new abode in hand, Grumble and Clara stepped into a world of luxury and comfort. The once homeless woman was now the mistress of a grand estate, thanks to the magic and determination of her goblin love.

The entrance foyer greeted them with marble floors that gleamed under the soft glow of chandeliers. Tall, arched windows framed views of lush gardens and a sun-drenched courtyard, a sight Clara could scarcely believe was hers to behold. She turned to Grumble, her eyes shimmering with gratitude.

"This... this is beyond anything I could have imagined," Clara whispered, her voice filled with wonder.

Grumble beamed, his eyes reflecting Clara's amazement. "It's all for you, my dear. Every stone, every beam, every petal in those gardens. This is our sanctuary, our haven."

Together, they explored room after room, each space more enchanting than the last. Grumble's touch was evident in the intricately carved woodwork, the whimsical tapestries, and the cozy nooks that seemed tailor-made for stolen moments of quiet reflection.

In the heart of the house, they found the grand library, a treasure trove of knowledge from countless realms. Clara's eyes danced over the shelves, her fingers trailing along the spines of books that held the promise of countless adventures.

"This," Clara breathed, "is a dream come true."

Grumble nodded, his heart swelling with pride. "I've collected these volumes from far and wide, hoping to provide you with a world of stories to lose yourself in."

As the days passed, Clara and Grumble settled into their new life of opulence and wonder. Clara's days were filled with exploration, her imagination ignited by the boundless possibilities of their new home.

Grumble reveled in the joy of seeing Clara thrive in this world he had crafted for her.

Their evenings were spent in the garden, surrounded by blooms of every color and scent. They dined under a sky filled with stars, their laughter mingling with the soft music of the night.

But amidst the luxury, Clara never forgot the journey that had brought them here. She often found herself stealing quiet moments in the garden, marveling at the twists of fate that had led her into Grumble's arms.

One evening, as the sun dipped below the horizon, casting the garden in a warm, golden hue, Clara turned to Grumble, her heart overflowing with love.

"This house, this life... it's more than I could have ever hoped for. But it's you, Grumble, who has truly given me a home."

Grumble took Clara's hand, his eyes filled with tenderness. "And it is you, my dearest Clara, who has given me a purpose, a reason to create this world of beauty and wonder."

In that moment, beneath the canvas of the evening sky, Clara and Grumble knew that their love had forged not just a home, but a legacy. This grand estate was not just a symbol of their newfound prosperity, but a testament to the power of love to shape and transform lives.

As they stood hand in hand, ready to face the adventures that awaited them in this new chapter of their lives, Clara and Grumble knew that their story was just beginning. Together, they would continue to fill the halls with laughter, the gardens with blooms, and their hearts with a love that knew no bounds.

As the seasons danced on, Clara and Grumble's home became a sanctuary not only for themselves but for all who entered its opulent embrace. Friends and family gathered beneath its roof, and the laughter that echoed through its halls became the heartbeat of their shared existence.

The grand library, once a treasure trove of unexplored adventures, now held the stories of countless guests who sought solace among its shelves. Clara reveled in the joy of sharing her newfound haven with others, knowing that every book held the potential to transport them to another world.

In the garden, the blooms continued to flourish, painting the landscape with vibrant strokes of color. Clara's gentle touch and Grumble's green-thumbed care ensured that each petal was a testament to the love that flourished within those walls.

As the years passed, Clara's heart swelled with gratitude for the life they had built together. It was a life beyond her wildest dreams, a testament to the power of love to transform even the most humble beginnings into something extraordinary.

One cool autumn evening, as the leaves danced in the fading light, Clara and Grumble sat on their favorite bench in the garden, hands intertwined. Clara's gaze lingered on the house, its windows glowing warmly in the dusk.

"Grumble," she began, "do you remember when this was just a dream? When we stood on the precipice of uncertainty and took that leap of faith?"

Grumble's eyes twinkled with a mixture of nostalgia and contentment. "I do, my love. And look at us now, surrounded by the life we built together."

They sat in companionable silence, the echoes of their journey reverberating around them. Clara leaned into Grumble's side, her heart brimming with the knowledge that this was where she was meant to be.

Their story was one of magic, determination, and above all, boundless love. It was a story that had transformed not only their lives, but the lives of all who had been touched by their journey.

As the stars began to emerge in the indigo sky, Clara and Grumble knew that their adventure was far from over. With every passing day, their love deepened, their legacy grew, and their home continued to stand as a beacon of hope and possibility.

Hand in hand, they rose from the bench, ready to face whatever new chapters awaited them. Together, they would write a story that would endure for generations, a story of a love that had defied all odds and created a world of beauty and wonder.

And so, the years flowed by like a gentle river, carrying with them the echoes of laughter, the scent of blooming flowers, and the whispered secrets of the grand library. Clara and Grumble's love story became legend, a tale told in hushed tones around fires and shared with wide-eyed children.

Their home, once a mere building of stone and wood, had transformed into something more. It was a living entity, a testament to the power of love and the magic of shared dreams. It welcomed all who sought refuge within its walls, offering solace, inspiration, and a sense of belonging.

Generations came and went, each adding their own brushstroke to the ever-evolving tapestry of the estate. The blooms in the garden bore witness to countless weddings, and the halls echoed with the laughter of children, each new member of the family bringing their own unique spark to the legacy.

The grand library, now weathered by time and cherished by many, remained a sanctuary for those seeking solace in the written word. Clara's dream of sharing the magic of stories had become a reality, touching hearts and kindling imaginations.

As Clara and Grumble sat on their bench in the garden, the years etched upon their faces like gentle lines on a well-loved book, they looked upon their creation with hearts full of contentment.

"Our story, Grumble," Clara mused, "it's woven into every fiber of this place. Every stone, every book, every flower... they all hold a piece of us."

Grumble nodded, his gaze fixed on the house that had witnessed the entirety of their remarkable journey. "Indeed, my dear. This home is a living testament to the love that built it, and the dreams that continue to breathe life into its walls."

As the sun dipped below the horizon, casting a golden glow across the garden, Clara and Grumble turned towards the house, ready to embrace the warmth and comfort it offered. Their steps were steady, their hearts entwined, and their spirits filled with the knowledge that their legacy would endure long after they were gone.

Their story, a tale of magic, determination, and boundless love, would continue to inspire, to touch hearts, and to remind all who heard it that dreams, when nurtured with love, have the power to shape not only homes, but the very essence of life itself. And so, hand in hand, Clara and Grumble walked into the embrace of their beloved home, ready to face whatever new adventures awaited them in the chapters yet to be written.

Chapter 10: Building a Legacy

Inspired by their journey, Grumble and Clara set out to create an enterprise that would change lives. Their combined talents and unwavering dedication gave birth to a venture that blossomed beyond their wildest dreams.

Together, they founded the "Harmony Foundation," a non-profit organization dedicated to uplifting the lives of those in need. Drawing upon Grumble's innate sense of magic and Clara's boundless compassion, they sought to create a haven for the marginalized and downtrodden.

The foundation's first endeavor was a sanctuary for homeless individuals, a place where warm meals, clean beds, and a sense of belonging awaited those who had lost their way. Grumble used his magic to ensure the sanctuary was always safe and welcoming, its walls filled with an aura of comfort and hope.

Clara, with her gift for connecting with people, provided a listening ear and a kind word to all who sought solace within the sanctuary's walls. Her presence, imbued with the empathy born from her own struggles, offered a beacon of light in the darkest of times.

Word of the Harmony Foundation's work spread like wildfire, drawing volunteers, donors, and supporters from all walks of life. Together, they expanded their efforts, creating programs to provide education, job training, and mental health support to those in need.

As the foundation's reach extended far beyond their grand estate, Clara and Grumble knew that their venture had become a force for good in the world. The legacy they were building was not just about the bricks and mortar of their home, but about the lives they touched and the futures they transformed.

Years passed, and the Harmony Foundation continued to grow, its impact felt in cities and towns far and wide. Grumble and Clara, now revered for their tireless dedication, stood side by side as beacons of hope, proof that love and determination could shape the world.

One evening, as they walked hand in hand through the sanctuary's garden, Clara turned to Grumble, her eyes shining with pride.

"Grumble, look at what we've created. This foundation is changing lives, just as you changed mine."

Grumble squeezed her hand, his heart full. "It's our legacy, my dearest Clara. A testament to the power of love and the boundless potential within each of us."

As the sun set, casting long shadows across the garden, Clara and Grumble knew that their story was no longer just their own. It was a story of resilience, of love's transformative power, and of the extraordinary heights humanity could reach when united by a shared dream.

With hearts full of gratitude, they walked back towards the grand estate, ready to face the challenges and joys that awaited them in the chapters still to come. Their legacy, forged in love and dedication, would continue to shape lives for generations to come, a living testament to the magic of their shared journey.

In the golden twilight of their years, Clara and Grumble's hearts swelled with a deep sense of fulfillment. Their legacy, the Harmony Foundation, had become a living embodiment of the change that love and compassion could bring to the world.

Every day, they saw the impact of their work etched in the smiles of those they helped. The homeless found shelter, families were reunited, and individuals discovered their own strength and resilience. The foundation's reach extended far and wide, touching lives across cities and continents.

As Clara stood before the gathered community, her voice steady and filled with purpose, she knew that their journey was far from over. "Together, we have shown that love is the greatest force for transformation. We have witnessed lives rebuilt, dreams rekindled, and a future of boundless potential emerge from the shadows of adversity."

Grumble, standing by her side, looked out at the faces before them, a tapestry of hope and resilience. "Each one of you is a testament to the power of the human spirit, and to the love that binds us all."

As the years flowed by, Clara and Grumble's estate continued to be a haven for those seeking refuge and renewal. The grand library, once a sanctuary of stories, now held the histories of those whose lives had been touched by the Harmony Foundation.

One evening, in the warmth of their home, Clara turned to Grumble, her eyes filled with a quiet contentment. "Our legacy, Grumble, it's a symphony of lives transformed. I never imagined our journey would lead us here."

Grumble smiled, his eyes reflecting the firelight. "And yet, my love, here we stand, at the heart of a movement that has touched countless souls. Our legacy is not just in the foundation, but in every life it has touched."

As the years turned into decades, Clara and Grumble knew that their time in this world was drawing to a close. They faced it with grace, knowing that the foundation they had built would continue to flourish in the hands of those they had inspired.

One evening, as the sun set in a blaze of oranges and purples, Clara and Grumble stood together in their beloved garden, the place where their journey had truly begun. They looked out at the grand estate, at the sanctuary, and at the lives that had been forever changed.

"Our story, Grumble," Clara said softly, "it's a tale of love, of transformation, of building something greater than ourselves."

Grumble nodded, his heart swelling with pride. "And it will continue to echo through the ages, a reminder that love is the greatest force for change."

As the final rays of sunlight faded, Clara and Grumble turned and walked hand in hand towards their home. They knew that their legacy, forged in love and compassion, would continue to shape the world long after they were gone. And as they entered the embrace of their beloved estate, they did so with hearts full of gratitude, knowing that their story would live on in the lives they had touched.

Chapter 11: The Wedding Bells

In a grand celebration, Grumble and Clara exchanged vows, surrounded by the friends and allies who had supported them along the way. Their love story, once shrouded in mystery and magic, was now a the brightestbeacon of hope and inspiration.

The grand estate, adorned with vibrant blooms and lit with a thousand candles, seemed to shimmer with its own joy. The air was filled with the fragrance of fresh flowers and the melodic notes of a string quartet. It was a day of pure enchantment, a day that marked the culmination of their extraordinary journey.

Clara, radiant in a gown woven with threads of silver and lace, walked down the aisle with a grace that seemed to defy gravity. Her eyes, aglow with love, met Grumble's, who stood at the altar, resplendent in a tailored suit that matched the grandeur of the occasion.

As Clara reached Grumble's side, they exchanged a glance that spoke volumes. It was a look that said, "We made it. We built this life together." Their hands found each other's, fingers intertwining in a silent pledge of love and forever.

The ceremony was officiated by a wise old sage, a friend they had met on their early travels, who had witnessed the blossoming of their love. His words, filled with wisdom and warmth, spoke of the power of love to shape destinies and build legacies.

Vows were exchanged, each promise a testament to the depth of their devotion. They vowed to stand by each other's side through all of life's adventures, to support and cherish, to build a future filled with shared dreams.

As they sealed their vows with a kiss, the grand estate seemed to hold its breath, as if in awe of the love that radiated from the newlyweds. And then, the garden erupted in a chorus of cheers and applause, a symphony of joy that echoed through the halls.

The celebration that followed was a testament to the bonds they had forged. Friends, family, and allies from all walks of life came together to honor the love that had inspired them all. The banquet tables were laden with the finest delicacies, and the air was filled with laughter and music.

As the night unfolded, Clara and Grumble stole moments together, their hearts brimming with gratitude for the love that had carried them through every twist and turn. They danced under the starlit sky, their steps a reflection of the harmonious life they had built.

When the final notes of the evening's music faded into the night, Clara and Grumble stood together on a balcony, gazing out at the grand estate that had witnessed their entire journey. The night was filled with a sense of magic, as if the very stars above were celebrating with them.

"Our love story, Grumble," Clara murmured, "it's become a story for the ages."

Grumble's eyes twinkled with a mixture of pride and tenderness. "And it's a story that will continue to inspire generations to come."

Hand in hand, they turned and walked back into their grand estate, ready to face the new chapters that awaited them. The echoes of their celebration lingered in the air, a testament to the enduring power of love and the magic of their shared journey.

As the night deepened, Clara and Grumble stole away to a quiet alcove within their grand estate. The air was alive with the scent of blooming night-blooming jasmine, and the soft glow of lanterns illuminated their path.

Here, in the gentle embrace of the night, they found a moment of solitude amidst the joyous celebration. Clara turned to Grumble, her eyes filled with a profound sense of gratitude.

"This day, Grumble, it's more than I ever dared to dream. It's a testament to the love that has guided us, to the magic that has woven our story."

Grumble's hand found Clara's, his touch a reassurance of their shared journey. "It's a day of dreams fulfilled, my dearest Clara. And it's only the beginning."

They stood together, the echoes of their vows still ringing in their hearts. The night seemed to hold its breath, as if in reverence of the love that had blossomed within these walls.

In the distance, the soft strains of music serenaded them, a reminder of the celebration that awaited. But here, in this quiet moment, it was just Grumble and Clara, two souls bound by a love that had transcended worlds.

As the first light of dawn began to paint the horizon, Clara and Grumble returned to the festivities, hand in hand. The grand estate, now aglow with the first rays of morning, seemed to radiate with a quiet contentment.

The guests, still gathered in celebration, turned to welcome them back with smiles and embraces. The day had been a testament to the power of love, a symphony of joy that would echo through the ages.

As Clara and Grumble danced once more beneath the morning sun, they knew that this day would be etched into their hearts forever. It was a day of beginnings, of promises kept, and of a love that would continue to shape their story.

And as they looked out at the grand estate, at the gardens that had witnessed their journey, they knew that their love story, now woven into the very fabric of their home, would continue to inspire generations to come. Hand in hand, they faced the future, ready to embrace the new adventures that awaited them, knowing that their love was a force that could overcome any challenge, and that their legacy was one of boundless magic and enduring love.

As the sun cast its first golden rays over the grand estate, Clara and Grumble stood on the terrace, their hearts full of gratitude for the day that had brought them to this moment. The garden, still adorned with the remnants of the night's celebration, seemed to glow with a renewed vibrancy.

Clara turned to Grumble, her eyes shining with the promise of a thousand tomorrows. "This is our story, Grumble. A story of love, of magic, and of building a life together."

Grumble's gaze met hers, his eyes reflecting the morning light. "And it's a story that will continue to unfold, my dearest Clara. With every sunrise, we have a chance to create something new."

They descended from the terrace, hand in hand, ready to face the adventures that awaited them. The grand estate, now a living testament to their love, seemed to echo with the whispers of their shared journey.

In the days that followed, Clara and Grumble continued to pour their hearts into the Harmony Foundation, knowing that their legacy was not just in the grandeur of their home, but in the lives they touched through their work.

The seasons turned, and the grand estate witnessed the passage of time with grace. Each room held memories, each corner told a story, and the garden flourished under Clara's care and Grumble's magic.

And so, as the years flowed by, Clara and Grumble's love story continued to inspire. The grand celebration of their wedding day became a cherished memory, a reminder of the enduring power of love.

One evening, as they stood together on the balcony, watching the sun set over their beloved estate, Clara turned to Grumble, her heart full.

"Grumble, our love story is a tapestry woven with threads of magic and boundless devotion. It's a story I will treasure for all my days."

Grumble pulled her close, his arms a sanctuary of warmth and strength. "And I, my dearest Clara, am grateful for every moment of this extraordinary journey."

As the stars began to emerge in the darkening sky, Clara and Grumble knew that their legacy, built on love and compassion, would continue to shape the world. Hand in hand, they walked back into their grand estate, ready to face whatever new adventures awaited them.

Their love story, a beacon of hope and inspiration, would echo through the ages, reminding all who heard it that love, when nurtured with care and boundless determination, had the power to create a world of magic and enduring beauty.

Chapter 12: Sunset Years

In their golden years, Grumble and Clara looked back on a life well-lived. Their enterprise flourished, and their story became legend, inspiring generations to come.

The grand estate, now weathered by time and adorned with the patina of history, stood as a living testament to their enduring love. The gardens, once vibrant with the hues of youth, now held a quiet beauty, mirroring the wisdom that age had bestowed upon its caretakers.

Clara's once-dark hair now held streaks of silver, a crown of honor earned through the passage of time. Grumble's laughter lines told the story of a life filled with joy and purpose. Together, they moved through the grand halls with a grace that spoke of the countless years they had spent in each other's company.

Their enterprise, the Harmony Foundation, had grown beyond their wildest dreams. It was now a beacon of hope for countless souls, a sanctuary for those in need, and a force for good in a world that often craved compassion.

Generations of volunteers and supporters had joined their cause, carrying the torch of love and service that Clara and Grumble had ignited. The programs they had initiated continued to transform lives, leaving an indelible mark on the communities they served.

One autumn afternoon, as the leaves rustled in the gentle breeze, Clara and Grumble sat in their favorite alcove, hands entwined. They watched as the sun painted the garden in hues of gold and amber, a reflection of the beauty that had graced their lives.

"Our story, Grumble," Clara began, "it's become a tapestry woven with threads of love and service. I'm grateful for every moment, every challenge, and every triumph."

Grumble turned to her, his eyes filled with a warmth that had only deepened with the years. "And I, my dearest Clara, am grateful for you.

For your love, your strength, and your unwavering belief in the power of kindness."

As the sun began its descent, casting long shadows across the garden, Clara and Grumble knew that their time in this world was a precious gift. They had lived a life of purpose, a life that had touched countless others.

In the years that followed, Clara and Grumble's love story became the stuff of legend. It was told around hearths and shared in whispered conversations. Their names were synonymous with compassion, their legacy a testament to the enduring power of love.

And as they faced the sunset years together, Clara and Grumble did so with hearts full of gratitude. They knew that their story, woven with threads of magic and boundless devotion, would continue to inspire generations to come.

Hand in hand, they walked through the grand estate, ready to face whatever came their way. The echoes of their journey reverberated through the halls, a reminder that their love had shaped not only their own lives, but the lives of all who had been touched by their story.

And so, as the sun dipped below the horizon, casting a warm golden glow over their haven, Clara and Grumble knew that their adventure was ongoing, that there were still new chapters waiting to be written. With hearts full of gratitude, they looked forward to whatever the future held, knowing that as long as they faced it together, their story would continue to be one of beauty, of love, and of a legacy fulfilled.

In the twilight of their lives, Clara and Grumble found solace in the embrace of their beloved estate. Every corner held memories, every whispering breeze seemed to carry echoes of their laughter.

As the years passed, their love had grown deeper, transcending the bounds of mortal existence. They often spoke without words, their hearts entwined in a dance of shared understanding.

One winter's eve, with the snow gently blanketing the garden, they sat on their favorite bench, hands clasped in a silent communion. The air was filled with a serene stillness, as if nature itself held its breath in reverence of their love.

Clara turned to Grumble, her eyes sparkling with the wisdom of a lifetime. "Our journey, Grumble, it's been a tapestry woven with threads of love and purpose. Every moment, every struggle, it was all worth it."

Grumble's gaze held a soft intensity, a reflection of the profound connection that bound them. "You've been the beacon of my existence, Clara. Your love has been the guiding light, illuminating even the darkest of days."

In that moment, as the snowflakes kissed their cheeks, they knew that their time together in this realm was drawing to a close. They had lived a life of meaning, a life that had touched the hearts of countless souls.

As the night deepened, Clara and Grumble returned to their grand estate, its walls holding the echoes of a lifetime of love. They ascended to their chamber, where they lay down side by side, hands still entwined.

With the first light of dawn, as the sun painted the horizon in hues of gold, Grumble's hand grew still in Clara's grasp. His gaze, filled with a serene acceptance, met Clara's tearful eyes.

"Thank you, my love," he whispered, his voice a gentle breeze that brushed against her soul.

Clara held him close, her heart breaking and expanding in the same breath. "Thank you, Grumble, for a life beyond my wildest dreams."

As the sun rose, casting a warm glow over the grand estate, Clara sat by Grumble's side, watching as his form slowly faded into the morning light.

In the quiet stillness, she knew that their love was eternal, a flame that would burn on through the ages. Grumble had become a part of the very fabric of her being, a presence that would guide her steps, even in his absence.

With a heart heavy with loss and a spirit buoyed by the love they had shared, Clara rose from their chamber, ready to face a world forever changed. She knew that Grumble's legacy, their legacy, would continue to inspire and uplift, just as it had always done.

And so, as the sun bathed their grand estate in a golden embrace, Clara walked forward, carrying with her the enduring love that had defined her existence. Grumble's spirit danced in the sunlight, a silent promise that they would meet again in the tapestry of eternity.

Generations passed, and the tale of Grumble and Clara became a cherished legend, passed down through time. Parents whispered the story to their children, and those children, in turn, to their own.

The city itself seemed to hold their memory close, as if the very stones remembered the goblin who had once roamed its alleys, and the woman whose life he had forever transformed.

In the hearts of those who heard their story, the spark of magic and the belief in the extraordinary burned bright. Acts of kindness and selflessness echoed through the years, a living testament to the love that had once blossomed between a goblin and a homeless woman.

And so, as the sun set on one chapter, it rose on another. The legacy of Grumble and Clara continued to shape the world, an enduring testament to the power of love to transcend all boundaries, even those between worlds.

Epilogue

A Legacy of Magic and Love:

In the realm beyond, Grumble and Clara found solace in each other's arms, their spirits intertwined in an eternal embrace. From their vantage point among the stars, they gazed down at the world they had touched, a world forever changed by their extraordinary journey.

Their legacy lived on, woven into the fabric of the city they had called home. The enterprise they had built thrived, a testament to their vision, determination, and the boundless power of love.

www.ingramcontent.com/pod-product-compliance
Lightning Source LLC
Chambersburg PA
CBHW031133160726
47989CB00017B/2907